SCRATCH
and the
GHOST SHIP

For more exciting adventures with

SCRATCH KITTEN

look out for . . .

Scratch Kitten Goes to Sea

Scratch Kitten on the Pirate's Shoulder

Scratch Kitten and the Ragged Reef

Scratch Kitten and the Terrible Beasties

Scratch Kitten and the Treasure Island

SCRATCH KITTEN
and the
GHOST SHIP

JESSICA GREEN • MITCH VANE

LITTLE HARE
www.littleharebooks.com

For Tricia—JG

For my lovely Katz and Kittens—MV

Little Hare Books
8/21 Mary Street, Surry Hills
NSW 2010 AUSTRALIA

www.littleharebooks.com

Text copyright © Jessica Green 2010
Illustrations copyright © Mitch Vane 2010

First published in 2010

National Library of Australia
Cataloguing-in-Publication entry

Green, Jessica.

Scratch Kitten and the ghost ship / Jessica Green ;
illustrator, Mitch Vane.

978 1 921541 07 0 (pbk.)

For primary school age.

Vane, Mitch.

A823.4

Cover design by Lore Foye
Set in 17/24 pt Bembo by Clinton Ellicott
Printed by Griffin Press
Printed in Adelaide, Australia, November 2009

5 4 3 2 1

Contents

How It All Began

Scratch was a ship's cat. He had found Mrs Captain's diamonds and he'd found his Paa. But instead of being happy, he was sad and frightened. Paa and Mrs Captain had sailed away, leaving Scratch alone on a tiny island in the middle of the ocean.

Scratch prowled along the beach.

He hoped his friends would come back for him. But all night long, the only sound he heard was swishing waves.

Just as the sun rose, Scratch heard voices. He pricked up his ears.

A rowboat pulled up on the beach. Four men climbed out and ran off with buckets to find fresh water.

A short man, who looked like he was the captain, scowled at the island.

'This isn't the Great South Land!' he growled. 'It's just an island. We'll get water and return straight to the ship.'

A tall, thin and sad-looking young man in purple boots with high heels was holding a bundle of empty sacks. 'No we won't!' he said. 'I can see some unusual shrubs, and I want to collect them.'

Scratch bounded down the sand. He climbed straight up the captain's leg and onto his shoulder.

'What are you doing here all by yourself, little cat?' cried the captain.

The thin man glared at Scratch.

'It was probably marooned here for being a pest, Captain Crank,' he said.

'Nonsense, Sir Peter,' said the captain, tickling Scratch under the chin. 'I'll take him on board the *South Seas Explorer*. We need a ship's cat.'

'I don't care where you're going!' Scratch mewed. 'So long as I can come too!'

Sir Peter stalked away. 'No one listens to *me*!' he spluttered. 'But I'll show you all. And I will show Father! I'll be famous, just you wait.'

He started breaking flowers and seed pods from some bushes at the end of the beach. 'It's a new plant!' he shouted back to the captain.

'I'll name it Peter's Peculiar Plant!'

The other men came stumbling back with their water buckets.

'We're setting off,' Captain Crank yelled.

'You will go when I say so!' shouted Sir Peter. 'Don't forget, I'm paying for this voyage!'

The captain groaned. He put Scratch into the rowboat and went to help Sir Peter collect more pods and flowers.

At last, Sir Peter and the captain brought the bulging sacks to the boat and loaded them on board.

'These specimens are splendid!' Sir Peter said. 'And *I* saw them first, before anyone in the world!'

'But I already saw those yesterday!' Scratch mewed.

'Be quiet, you caterwauling creature!' said Sir Peter. 'And stay clear of my specimens.'

Scratch slunk to the prow of the rowboat. 'I'm in trouble already,' he thought. 'But it doesn't matter. So long as I'm on a ship, and not marooned on a deserted island.'

1.

Scratch Finds a Friend

The sailors rowed out into the bay where the ship was waiting. Then they hoisted Sir Peter with his bags of flowers, pods and seeds onto the deck. Scratch scrambled aboard and ran straight to the ship's rail, where he wouldn't be in the way. He watched the men set the sails. His nostrils twitched as he sniffed the air.

'What's that earthy smell?' he wondered.

Once the ship was sailing away from the island, Scratch jumped down to explore. He found some barrels lined up along the ship's sides. They were all filled with soil. Some had spindly plants growing in them. He jumped to the rim of the nearest barrel.

'Why are these here?' he wondered. 'Maybe they belong to that flower man, Sir Peter.'

Two sailors came staggering along the deck, hauling a pile of sails between them. One was hairy all over, except on top of his head. The other was strong and thin, but had only one arm. They bumped against Scratch's barrel as they passed. The barrel rocked, and the plant and some soil spilled onto the deck.

'You clumsy clot, Hairy Joe!' cried the one-armed man. 'Sir Peter Petall will stick us headfirst in that barrel for this!'

'It was an accident, Deckhand Dave!' said the other. 'Let's scram before he sees the mess we've made!'

The men staggered away. Scratch was about to scram too, when he heard a snuffling sound. He jumped down to investigate. The sound came from behind a stack of boxes. Scratch crept towards the boxes and found a bamboo cage. Inside was an odd creature. It was the size of a cat, with long ears and a long tail like a monkey. But instead of being furry, it had smooth, shiny skin. The stripes on its skin were the exact same colour as the slats of the bamboo cage.

Scratch sniffed through the slats.

The strange creature shrank back, popeyed. 'What sort of a weird creature are you?' it asked.

'I'm Scratch, the new ship's cat,' said Scratch. 'Who are you?'

'I call myself Toopo,' the creature snuffled. 'But the man calls me Peter's Poly-Pussum.'

'Which man?' asked Scratch.

'The collecting man, Sir Peter!' said Toopo. 'He collected me from the island where I lived. I was the only one there. He's taking me away!' Toopo sniffed. 'He says I'm a lizard-skinned cat! He's going to put me in a glass case so people can *stare* at me! How will I find my true love if I'm in a glass case?'

'I don't like Sir Peter!' squeaked
Scratch. 'I'm going to find myself
another ship with no Sir Peter on
board. You can come too, if you like,
and find your true love.'

'Will you protect me?' said Toopo.

'Oh . . . er,' said Scratch. He hadn't
thought about that. 'I suppose so.

I'm good at saving and protecting.
There was this parrot——'

'You don't *have* to help me,'
snuffled Toopo. 'Sir Peter might put
you in a glass case too!'

'I've rescued a parrot, and I've
rescued a captain,' said Scratch, 'so I
could probably save a Poly-Pussum.'

Scratch set to work chewing and
clawing at the cord that tied the cage
door. He kept going until his teeth
and claws hurt. The cord frayed, but
still held fast.

'This is hard work,' said Scratch.

Toopo lay on his back. 'I'm
doomed!' he moaned.

Just then they heard footsteps.
It was Sir Peter.

Scratch clawed harder. Suddenly the cord snapped. The cage door sprang open. Sir Peter's shadow loomed over the barrels. Toopo burst out, and ducked behind the boxes. Scratch was about to follow, when he was pinned to the deck by a purple boot.

'What have you done with my Peter's Poly-Pussum?' cried Sir Peter.

Scratch twisted out from under Sir Peter's boot and squeezed between two barrels.

'Just you wait, you fusty feline!' yelled Sir Peter. 'I'll get you!'

2.

Scratch Tries to Help

Scratch prowled the deck, searching for Toopo. He looked under benches, behind barrels and inside folded sails. He looked below decks and among the stores.

'Where are you, Toopo?' he mewed. 'I hope you haven't fallen overboard.'

He couldn't find Toopo anywhere.

In the end he gave up and padded back to Sir Peter's barrels and boxes. At first he didn't notice the dirt and uprooted flowers on the deck.

Suddenly he heard a snuffle.

'Hello, Scratch!'

Scratch looked up and saw Toopo in one of the barrels, eating a worm. Strangely, Toopo was no longer the colour of bamboo. Now he was the same colour as the soil he sat on.

'Oh, Toopo!' Scratch yowled. 'Look at the mess! When Sir Peter finds this he'll be furious!'

'I'm so hungry!' snuffled Toopo. 'My proper food is purple flowers, but Sir Peter doesn't know that. So I've dug up some worms. I hate worms.'

'You'd better hide again!' said
Scratch. 'I'll try to clean up.'

Toopo jumped down and watched
while Scratch tried to scrape the soil
out through one of the scuppers.
This time, neither of them heard
Sir Peter creeping up behind them.

Suddenly there was a screech.

Scratch froze. Toopo darted between two barrels. His skin changed colour so it blended with the boards of the deck.

'You little beast!' Sir Peter cried. 'Now you've killed my Puffy Pink-Peter-Plant!'

Captain Crank bustled out of his cabin to see what the commotion was about. Hairy Joe and Deckhand Dave peered around the mast, and Eagle-eye Eric leaned out of the crow's nest to stare.

'Either that animal goes, or I do!' Sir Peter cried.

'The cat spilled some dirt, that's all,' the captain growled.

'It dug up my plant!' Sir Peter

howled. 'It ate my Peter's Poly-Pussum! It must go!'

The captain lifted Scratch onto his shoulder. 'Nonsense, Sir Peter! If your silly pots were stashed below decks, then there'd be no trouble.'

Sir Peter stamped his foot. 'How *dare* you call my work silly! I'm paying for this trip! I insist you dismiss that cat!'

'No one is dismissed,' the captain grunted. 'Hairy Joe, make Sir Peter some tea.'

'I don't want tea!' cried Sir Peter. 'I want my Poly-Pussum!' He stormed below decks to his cabin and slammed the door so hard that even Eagle-eye Eric heard it in the crow's nest.

Dave and Joe laughed until they rolled on the deck. Up in the rigging, Mighty Mick, who was the shortest man Scratch had ever seen, laughed so hard he nearly fell off. Whitebeard Wal, a bent old sailor whose job it was to keep the ropes tidy, laughed so much he got all tangled up.

'Quit laughing!' the captain boomed. 'Sir Peter is right. He paid for this trip. So stick that weed back in the barrel and get back to work, or we'll never find the Great South Land.'

'Aye, aye, Captain,' chortled the sailors.

The captain went to finish his charts. 'I knew Sir Peter was a pain in the neck,' he muttered as he went, 'but I'd never have taken this trip if I'd known he was this bad!'

Scratch sighed. 'I'll leave this ship at the very next port,' he thought. 'And I'll take Toopo with me! I won't let Sir Peter put my friend in a glass case!'

He jumped down from the captain's shoulder and scampered off to tell Toopo. There was no sign of his new friend, but one of the rope coils smelled strongly of him.

'Toopo?' he mewed. 'Are you hiding under there?'

There was no answer. 'Perhaps he's too scared to answer,' Scratch thought. 'Come out!' he mewed. 'Let's plan our escape!'

But Toopo did not appear.

3.

The Ghost Ship

As Scratch sat on the ship's rail waiting for Toopo, a sea mist rolled over the waves. Soon it was wafting around the ship. Scratch could hardly see his own whiskers.

Then something caught his eye.

'*Mee-ow!* What was that?'

Something big was out in the mist. Something ship-shaped.

'Ship ahoy!' he mewed.

He looked again. Nothing.

He blinked. There it was again!
A ship, looming through the mist.

It was old and unpainted. Ragged
brown sails hung limply from its
yardarms. There was not a single
sailor to be seen on board.

'*Ahoy!*' Scratch yowled.

No one hailed him from the ship.

It slipped silently past, then vanished, swallowed up by the mist.

Scratch rushed along the deck until he found a group of sailors.

'There's a ship out there,' he mewed, but they didn't listen.

'I wish I hadn't signed on,' said Hairy Joe. 'We can't see where we're going in this mist. We might fall off the edge of the world!'

'The real dangers are monsters,' said Mighty Mick, 'that come out when it's misty.'

'The worst are ghost ships,' muttered Whitebeard Wal. 'I hear there's one that sails around in the mist, with tattered sails and no crew.'

Everyone shuddered.

'I saw that ship!' Scratch yowled.

'Quiet, cat,' said Joe. 'Wal, tell us
what happens if we see one!'

Scratch wasn't interested in what
happened when you met a ghost ship.
He wanted to meet a *real* ship—and
get on board it as soon as he could!
He trotted off to find Toopo and
make plans for their escape.

4.

Going Ashore

Scratch wasn't able to make any plans, because Toopo hid all night. Scratch slept on the deck, close to the rope that smelled of Toopo.

He was woken at dawn.

'Land ho!' cried Eric from the crow's nest.

Captain Crank stumbled from his cabin. 'Land?' he croaked sleepily.

'Have we found the mysterious Great South Land?'

The sailors crowded onto the deck and hung over the rails. They were so excited about the Great South Land, they forgot all about falling off the edge of the world. Scratch kept his eyes peeled for a harbour or port where he and Toopo could go ashore.

A few hours later, the *South Seas Explorer* anchored in a sheltered bay. Scratch was worried. Toopo still hadn't appeared. Here was a chance

to escape, but he couldn't leave without Toopo. He sat on the rail and studied the coastline. He saw beaches, bushes, and rocky crags. But there was no sign of a port.

'What if this is another deserted island?' thought Scratch. 'What if the love of Toopo's life doesn't live here? I'd better take a look around and make an escape plan. I can tell Toopo later, when I find him.'

The crew lowered the rowboat.

Scratch didn't want Sir Peter to see him tagging along, so he crawled under a specimen bag that was packed inside one of Sir Peter's baskets. Moments later he was lowered into the rowboat.

Once they were on the beach, Captain Crank spent the afternoon measuring the sandhills and taking notes so he could make a map. Hairy Joe, Deckhand Dave and Mighty Mick went searching for fresh water. Sir Peter collected plants on the sand dunes. His pile of seed pods and flowers grew bigger and bigger.

Scratch climbed the highest sand dune to look for a town with a port, but all he could see were more dunes.

And all he could hear were the
crashing waves, and Sir Peter talking
to himself.

'I'll bet Father has never been here,'
Sir Peter muttered. 'I'll bet Father has
never found what I've found.'

'No port here!' Scratch thought.
'But there *is* a shrub with purple
flowers for Toopo!'

Sir Peter saw the shrub at the same time. But he didn't look at the flowers. He looked at the spotted butterflies that sat on the flowers.

'Those butterflies will look perfect in a frame!' said Sir Peter, getting his butterfly net ready. 'Father will be so proud when he sees them.'

Scratch though how happy Toopo would be to have some flowers to eat. 'I'll pick some flowers for him!' he mewed, and leapt into the shrub.

A moment later, all the butterflies had flown away.

'You dratted cat!' howled Sir Peter, throwing the net at Scratch.

Scratch jumped sideways and landed in Sir Peter's pile of specimens.

Their stems snapped and their petals crumpled.

Sir Peter threw himself on the ground. 'You're ruining everything!' he shrieked.

Captain Crank lumbered up the dune. 'What's the ruckus?' he panted. He dragged Sir Peter to his feet. 'Why fuss about a kitten? We've found the Great South Land!'

'I was only picking flowers for Toopo,' Scratch explained.

'Make it stop yowling!' shrieked Sir Peter. 'I order you to leave it behind!'

'It's just a little cat!' the captain said. 'I know you're an important passenger, but *I* am captain, and *I* say who gets left behind.'

The captain helped Sir Peter carry his specimen bags and baskets back to the rowboat. Then the men put Scratch on board, loaded the water barrels and got the oars ready.

Sir Peter pointed a shaking finger at Scratch. But he was so furious he couldn't think of a single thing to say.

Scratch hid behind the captain's boots. He almost wished he *was* being left behind—but not on a lonely beach with no port and no new ship to join. And not without Toopo.

'I don't care if this is the Great South Land,' he thought to himself. 'I just want to be a happy ship's cat on a happy ship.'

5.

Sir Peter Plots

Next morning it was misty again.

Scratch washed his tail for a long
time. Washing helped him think.
'There's no sign of a port!' he
thought. 'If Toopo and I don't escape
soon, Sir Peter will put us both in a
glass case! Then I'll never be a ship's
cat again, and Toopo will never find
his true love.'

He didn't hear Sir Peter tiptoe up
behind him in his purple boots.

Suddenly Sir Peter snatched up
Scratch by the scruff of his neck.

'*Mee-ouch!*' Scratch yowled.

Sir Peter shook him. 'This was
a fine trip until you came along!'
he hissed. 'I'd throw you overboard,
but Captain Crank would be angry.'

Scratch struggled.

Sir Peter gripped harder. 'So it's about time you had a sad accident!' he snarled. 'And sad accidents often happen when there's a mist.'

Suddenly there was a shout from the crow's nest.

'Ship to starboard!' cried Eric.

Mighty Mick and Deckhand Dave ran to the rail. Whitebeard Wal and Hairy Joe followed.

'It's gone again!' Eric yelled.

'Look! Over there!' Wal gasped.

Captain Crank stormed out of his cabin.

Sir Peter dropped Scratch on a coil of rope and hurried across the deck to join the sailors.

Scratch landed on something soft.
The thing wriggled and squirmed.

It was Toopo!

'Sorry, Toopo,' said Scratch.
'Where did you pop up from?'

'Nowhere,' snuffled Toopo. 'I've
been here all along.'

'I didn't see you!' mewed Scratch.

'I was hiding so nobody could see
me,' said Toopo.

'But . . . when I first saw you, your skin looked like the slats of your bamboo cage. Now it looks like a coil of rope! How do you do that?'

'It's how I hide,' said Toopo. 'I'm a sort of chameleon.'

'Well, don't hide again,' said Scratch. 'Eric has spotted a ship. If we're lucky, we might be able to stow away on it and escape from Sir Peter. I'll take a look. You stay here.'

Scratch trotted across the deck and jumped onto the ship's rail.

He saw a deserted ship with ragged sails and no paint. The masts creaked and the ropes swayed.

'Ahoy there!' Captain Crank roared. 'Show your colours!'

No one called back.

Hairy Joe's hair stood on end.

'It's the ghost ship!' he cried.

'We're doomed!' moaned Mighty Mick.

'That's the ship I saw before!' mewed Scratch.

Nobody listened to him.

'It's just an old ship,' said the captain.

Nobody listened to him either.

Sir Peter scowled and stamped his foot. 'I know that stupid ship,' he muttered to himself. 'I should have known! Now my plans are ruined.'

The ship slipped into the mist.

Deckhand Dave crouched in terror on the deck. Hairy Joe and Mighty Mick hugged each other.

'There are no ghosts!' boomed Captain Crank. 'And no ghost ships!'

'Then where is the crew?' whispered Mick.

'They must be having breakfast,' said the captain. 'Now, all hands on deck. We're sailing south.'

'Ahem . . . that's where the . . . er . . . ghost ship is headed!' said Sir Peter.

'That's right,' said Captain Crank. 'We're going to follow it and see what's going on.'

'But I don't *want* to see what's going on!' snapped Sir Peter. 'Besides . . . that's the stupid . . . I mean, that's the scary *Petunia May*.'

'Not the *Petunia May*!' gasped Wal.

'That's right,' said Sir Peter. 'The ...
er ... unluckiest ghost ship of them
all. No good can come of following
the *Petunia May*.'

'Stop talking nonsense!' growled
the captain. Then he yelled up to the
crow's nest. 'Report any sighting of
that ship, Eagle-eye Eric. It needs
investigating. As for the rest of you,

the wind's coming up! Trim the sails and steer south-west!'

Scratch jumped down from the rail and ran back to Toopo. 'I think Sir Peter knows something about the *Petunia May*. But he's trying to scare the men!' he mewed. 'I don't understand!'

'He scares everyone,' snuffled Toopo. 'Especially me!'

The crew did their best to follow the captain's orders. But their hands shook so hard that they knotted ropes loosely and fastened sails badly. When they tried to steer south-west they couldn't keep the ship straight. The ship shuddered and lurched all night long.

6.

Another Visit Ashore

There was no wind or mist the next morning, and no ghost ship. But there was a long line of green coast. It was edged with rocky cliffs and golden beaches.

Sir Peter sat at a table on the deck, near his boxes and barrels, and pressed flowers between layers of paper. He didn't know that Toopo was crouched near his feet. Topoo was invisible because his skin was now the colour of the boxes he was hiding behind. Scratch huddled with Toopo to make sure he stayed safe.

'Why do we have to follow the *Petunia May*?' Sir Peter muttered to himself. 'I don't want to see Father until I'm famous!'

'What is Sir Peter talking about?' snuffled Toopo.

'He's been like this ever since he saw the ghost ship,' said Scratch.

Suddenly Eagle-eye Eric yelled from the crow's nest. 'Look at those parrots!' he shouted.

Sir Peter jumped up, dropping his flowers on the deck. 'Where? What?' he cried. 'I saw them first!'

Scratch stuck his head through a scupper and gazed up and down the coast. 'All I can see are beaches and cliffs and trees,' he whispered to Toopo. 'There must be a town and a port somewhere.'

'Don't forget the love of my life,' snuffled Toopo.

'Drop anchor, boys!' cried the captain. 'Lower the rowboat. Sir Peter wants to collect those parrots.'

Sir Peter rushed to pick up his bags. The sailors loaded the rowboat with empty barrels, bags and baskets.

Toopo scrambled out of hiding to eat Sir Peter's dropped flowers. His skin turned pink and yellow and green as he chewed on the petals.

'Wait here,' Scratch told Toopo, 'while I go ashore and see if this is a good place to escape.'

Sir Peter came rushing back. Toopo froze, and the colours of his skin made him invisible among the scattered flowers. Sir Peter saw only Scratch sitting among the remains of the flowers that Toopo had eaten.

'You've ruined my flowers!' Sir Peter cried.

He dropped his bags, snatched Scratch and dangled him over the rail. 'You're wrecking my trip!' he screamed. 'I don't care if Captain Crank sees me getting rid of you. It's time for you to take a swim!'

Scratch wriggled and hissed.

Toopo's skin turned from pink and yellow to angry scarlet. He threw himself at Sir Peter and latched his claws and teeth into Sir Peter's leg.

'*Aaaaah!*' Sir Peter screeched.

Scratch fell to the deck.

Sir Peter spotted Toopo. 'My Peter's Poly-Pussum!' he shouted. 'It's alive!'

Toopo ran away. Sir Peter crawled after him. Toopo scuttled onto a sail and turned white. Sir Peter lunged at him. Toopo ducked behind Scratch and turned ginger. Sir Peter swiped Scratch out of the way. Toopo crept between two barrels and turned brown. Sir Peter dived after him ... and got stuck.

'Get me out!' he screeched.

Hairy Joe and Captain Crank heard the fuss and came running from the rowboat. They each took a leg and pulled. The barrels tipped, spilling soil and plants. Sir Peter sat up, holding Toopo by the tail.

'So the cat *didn't* eat it?' asked Joe.

'Er ... no,' muttered Sir Peter.

He stuffed Toopo into a bag, and looked around for rope to tie it shut.

'Don't be long,' said Captain Crank, as he and Joe climbed down to the rowboat again. 'We can't wait all day to go ashore.'

'Alright, alright!' grumbled Sir Peter. 'Just wait while I pop the Poly-Pussum into its cage!'

'Don't be scared, Toopo!' mewed Scratch. 'I'll save you!'

He leapt bravely into the bag.

Quick as a flash, Sir Peter closed the bag, trapping both Scratch and Toopo inside. 'Gotcha!' he hissed.

Then Sir Peter thrust his hand into the bag to grab Toopo. Scratch bit his finger. Sir Peter gave the bag a shake.

Then he tried again. Toopo scratched
his wrist. Sir Peter grabbed Scratch
by the paw, and then by the tail.

'What are you doing?' yelled
Captain Crank from the rowboat.

'Nothing!' Sir Peter said.

At last Sir Peter caught Toopo
by his tail and pulled him out.
Then he tied the neck of the bag
shut so Scratch couldn't escape.

He put Toopo in his cage, tied it shut, and climbed into the rowboat with his bags.

Scratch was inside one of them.

'*Mee-owch!*' said Scratch.

'*Hum-hmmm-dum-de-dah!*' sang Sir Peter to drown out Scratch's mewing. '*Tra-la-la!*'

On shore, Captain Crank started measuring and mapping. The sailors looked for water, and Sir Peter left his empty specimen bags in the shade of some trees. Then he took the bag with Scratch inside, headed into the scrub and tossed the bag into a thicket.

'So long, you horrid little beast!' he said.

Then he trotted back to the beach.

Scratch wriggled and howled. 'Help!' he mewed.

He tried to claw a hole in the bag. Then he tried to chew a hole. It got hotter and hotter, and Scratch got more and more thirsty.

'*Miaow!*' he cried. 'Save me!'

After what seemed like hours, he heard heavy footsteps.

'Is that you, Captain Crank?' he mewed.

Captain Crank made a strange sound. *Boom! Boom!*

Suddenly Scratch felt himself being hoisted into the air. He was swung around, then dropped.

'*Youch!*' cried Scratch.

There was more swinging and dropping. The cord around the neck of the bag began to loosen. Then the bag, with Scratch inside, was swung about some more, dropped, picked up, shaken and dropped again.

At last the cord fell off. Scratch tumbled onto the ground.

BOOM BOOM BOOM

He twisted around and looked up.
An enormous bird peered down at
him. It had a bald head, long scaly
legs, huge feet and thin dangly
feathers. Its beak opened wide.

'Boom, boom, boom!' it said.

Scratch ran for his life.

He scampered to the beach. The
sailors were already heaving the
rowboat into the surf. Captain Crank
and Sir Peter were seated inside.

Scratch scrambled across the sand
and into the waves. He made a final
leap and landed on Sir Peter's lap.
Sir Peter nearly jumped out of his
britches. The boat rocked wildly.
Sir Peter's bags of specimens flew
into the air and fell overboard.

'My specimens!' Sir Peter shouted.

'Good grief!' the captain roared.

'How did the cat come to be on the shore?' cried Deckhand Dave.

'And how did he almost get left behind?' asked Hairy Joe.

Scratch shook water from his fur and leapt onto the captain's knees.

'Last time we saw him was on deck,' said Mighty Mick.

'He stowed away,' said Hairy Joe.

'Poor kitty!' said Deckhand Dave.

Sir Peter glared at Scratch. Scratch glared back.

'Just you wait,' hissed Sir Peter. 'No one comes between me and my plans!'

'No one comes between me and my plans, either,' mewed Scratch. 'I have to find a new ship, and the love of Toopo's life, as soon as I can!'

7.

Scratch in Strife

Sir Peter stormed straight to his cabin. 'No one understands me!' he cried over his shoulder. 'No one cares! You're all just like Father! Just you wait and see how famous I become. Then you'll be sorry!'

Scratch went to Toopo's cage. His friend was curled inside, his skin the colour of the bamboo slats.

'Stay away from me, Scratch!'
snuffled Toopo, when Scratch
told him what Sir Peter had done.
'It's safer for you!'

Scratch went away for a wash and a
think. Maybe he should just make a
dash for it as soon as they came across
another ship. But the more Scratch
thought, the more he knew that

Toopo needed someone to save him.
And that someone could only be
Scratch.

He went back to try and rescue
Toopo. But Toopo's cage was so
tightly roped that Scratch didn't
know where to start.

They could hear Sir Peter's voice
drifting up from his cabin porthole.
'Just you wait, you rotten lot!' he
shouted. 'I've discovered twenty-
three plants that no one has ever
discovered before. I'll be famous!
More famous than anyone!'

Sir Peter kept yelling all night.
No one else could sleep a wink
and everyone was tired and cranky.

By morning he had named seventy-four new plants. They all had the name 'Peter' in them.

Meanwhile, the ship kept sailing along the coast and rounded a headland.

'This land goes on forever!' Eagle-eye Eric shouted from the crow's nest. 'Is it still the Great South Land, or is it a new one?'

Sir Peter came storming up from his cabin. His hands and pockets were full of pods and flowers. Behind him lay a trail of seeds and petals.

'Did someone say a new land?' he shrieked. 'I saw it first! It is called *Peterland*! Take me ashore *now*!'

Just then Eagle-eye Eric croaked,
'Sh . . . sh . . . ship ahoy!'

On the far side of the headland
was a cove. And in the cove was a
ship. A silent, unpainted ship with
tattered sails.

Sir Peter went white and his knees
shook. 'It's the *Petunia May*!'
he moaned.

'Heave to, men!' yelled Captain Crank. 'We'll anchor right here!'

'No!' screeched Sir Peter.

The sailors crowded along the rail. Their knees knocked. 'That's the ghost ship,' they whispered.

Sir Peter stamped his foot. 'No one cares about me and what I want!' he wailed. 'I give up!'

He threw a basket of his specimens across the deck. It landed on Toopo's cage and bounced open. Then the open basket flew over the ship's rail, spilling specimens into the sea.

Sir Peter made a choking sound. He grabbed Toopo's cage, fell onto the deck and began to drum his heels on the boards.

8.

Aboard the Ghost Ship

The sailors were so terrified of the ghost ship, they could hardly steer their own ship towards it. But Captain Crank kept yelling at them, and at last the *South Seas Explorer* came alongside the *Petunia May*. Scratch jumped onto the rail and stared curiously at the peeling paintwork.

Sir Peter lay on the deck, clutching Toopo's cage to his chest and babbling nonsense. No one took any notice of him.

The sailors hid wherever they could.

'No good can come of this,' muttered Deckhand Dave.

'It ain't natural,' said Hairy Joe.

When Captain Crank ordered the sailors to prepare ropes to tie the *South Seas Explorer* to the *Petunia May*, they shook their heads.

'Get those ropes attached *now*!' roared the captain.

Whitebeard Wal and Mighty Mick shuffled forward. Their hands shook so hard, they dropped the ropes in the water.

In the end, Captain Crank had to fetch a gangplank himself and lay it across the gap between the two ships for boarding.

'Come along, Sir Peter,' he said.

'No!' squeaked Sir Peter.

'Come on, men!' called Captain Crank.

'I've got a tummy ache,' said Wal.

'Me too!' said Mick.

'And me,' added Joe.

'And me!' quavered Dave.

Scratch fluffed his fur with excitement. Maybe he and Topoo could stow away on the *Petunia May*. Perhaps this was the escape that he and Toopo were looking for . . . even if the sailors called it a ghost ship.

Captain Crank said there were no
such things as ghosts, so Scratch leapt
off the rail, bounded across the plank
and jumped straight onto the deck of
the *Petunia May*.

'I'll be back for you soon, Toopo,'
he called over his shoulder.

9.

The Ghosts

The *Petunia May*'s masts creaked. Her tattered sails flapped. There were no barrels or crates or coils of rope to be seen. There were no sailors swabbing the decks or working in the rigging. Scratch prowled along the deck. He reached a hatch and poked his nose in. His whiskers trembled and his fur stood on end.

'Captain Crank said there are no such things as ghosts,' Scratch reminded himself. 'And I can't *hear* any ghosts. So it *must* be a safe ship for me and Toopo. Just so long as I find some friendly sailors.'

Scratch crept slowly down the ladder. Below decks was empty too. A table was laid for a meal, with plates and tankards and knives. But no one sat to eat.

'Anybody home?' he mewed.

There was no reply.

Then Scratch froze.

There was something under the bench! He peered closer and saw six men. They lay head-to-toe against the wall, their hands over their faces.

'Ghosts!' mewed Scratch. 'Sleeping ghosts!'

He turned and raced back up the ladder, across the deck, over the rail, along the gangplank, and straight onto Captain Crank's shoulder.

'*Ghosts!*' Scratch yowled. 'Ghosts everywhere!'

'That cat has seen a ghost!' Wal quavered from behind a crate.

'Monsters!' shouted Dave from behind a cask.

'Giant octopus!' howled Mick from under a pile of sails.

'Mermaids!' squealed Hairy Joe.

'I want my mum!' yelled Eagle-eye Eric from the crow's nest.

'I want to go home,' Sir Peter whispered, still clutching Toopo's cage. 'I don't like collecting flowers after all.'

'Shame on you!' Captain Crank roared. 'This little cat is braver than everyone put together!'

Scratch didn't feel brave. He dug his claws into the captain's shoulder.

He didn't want to go back to the *Petunia May*. The sailors were right—it was a ghost ship. And Scratch knew that was no place for a creature like Topoo and a ginger kitten.

But when Captain Crank climbed onto the gangplank, Scratch's claws were so stuck in the captain's jacket that he couldn't let go. He had no choice but to go with him.

'Look at the state of this ship!' Captain Crank growled as he jumped onto the deck. 'My old granny could swab these decks better!'

Scratch clung harder as Captain Crank went down the hatch. It didn't take long for the captain to see what was under the bench.

He bent down and stared.

'I'd recognise those trousers anywhere,' he growled. 'Come out, Captain Kronk. And that purple coat belongs to Lord Florian, I presume?'

There were some groans and sighs. One by one, the six men rolled out and got to their feet. Scratch's eyes grew rounder and rounder. They weren't ghosts! They were real, living people!

'Why couldn't you just leave us alone?' said Lord Florian.

Scratch blinked. Lord Florian was a tall stooping gentleman with a familiar sad look on his face.

'We tried so hard to make the ship look like a ghost ship,' said Captain Kronk. 'Weren't you fooled?'

'Not me,' said Captain Crank. 'There are no such things as ghosts.'

'We hoped that if the *Petunia May* looked like a ghost ship,' said Lord Florian, 'everyone would think we had been lured onto the rocks by some mermaids.'

'Or swallowed by a giant octopus,'
added Captain Kronk.

'And then we would never have to
go home to our boring office jobs,'
said Lord Florian.

'We like sailing the South Seas,'
said Captain Kronk.

'And we don't like working in
offices,' said Lord Florian.

'If it had been up to my sailors,' said Captain Crank, 'we would have left you alone. You'll have to blame this brave little cat for ruining your secret.'

'Always the blasted cat!' whined a familiar voice.

There was a racket at the hatchway and Sir Peter struggled down the steps. He was laden with baskets, boxes, books and Toopo's bamboo cage. 'Hello, Daddy,' he said.

'Hello, son,' said Lord Florian.

Everyone made room as Sir Peter dumped everything on the table.

Scratch ran to Toopo's cage. 'Are you alright?' he mewed.

'I hope so,' snuffled Toopo.

'Do you think we'll find my lady love on this ship?'

'No,' said Scratch. 'But hopefully Lord Florian will let us sail with him. And then we might come across an island where your lady love lives.'

'Daddy, you'll be so proud of me,' said Sir Peter. 'I've discovered many things!'

'Did you discover this brave cat too?' asked Lord Florian.

Sir Peter glared at Scratch.

'It discovered us,' said Captain Crank.

'This is Peter's Prickly Plant,' Sir Peter said, and waved a dead stick in the air. 'It was perfect until the cat ruined it.'

'I already discovered that plant,' said Lord Florian. 'I named it Florian's Formidable Foliage.'

'Well, here's my Purple Peter-rose!' Sir Peter said.

'No, that one's called Violet Florian-flower,' said Lord Florian.

Every plant Sir Peter showed them, Lord Florian had already discovered— and named after himself!

'What silly names!' muttered Sir Peter. Then he pointed at Toopo. 'This is my Peter's Poly-Pussum. It's a Polynesian Lizard-skinned Marsupial Cat,' he said proudly.

'Actually, that's a Tahitian Lizard-skinned Flower-eating Chameleon-mammal,' said Lord Florian. 'I've got a female one. Her name is Florrie.'

Scratch nearly jumped out of his skin. 'Did you hear that, Toopo?' he squeaked. 'There's a lady Toopo on this ship!'

Toopo turned as pale as a ghost. 'Oh, my!' he snuffled. 'I've never met a lady before. What shall I say to her?'

Tears rolled down Sir Peter's cheeks. 'The Poly-Pussum was my best discovery!' he sniffed. 'I was going to put it in a glass case.'

'A glass case!' cried Lord Florian, horrified. 'Why would you do that?'

Sir Peter wasn't listening. 'So you still don't love me, Daddy?' he whimpered. 'After I tried so hard.'

'Of course I do,' Lord Florian said.

Sir Peter blew his nose into a huge hanky. 'I don't believe you,' he said.

'I'll prove it to you,' Lord Florian said. 'Why don't you take my collection home? You can tell everyone we discovered it together.'

Sir Peter's eyes almost popped out of his head. 'But what about you?'

'I don't want to go home,' said
Lord Florian. 'I prefer sailing.'

'Me too,' said Captain Kronk. 'But
it will be better if we don't have to be
a *ghost ship* any more. I'm too old for
hiding under benches.'

'Oh, thanks, Daddy!' Sir Peter
gasped. 'I'll take our Poly-Pussums
back to my ship right away!'

'Actually,' said Lord Florian, 'the Chameleon-mammals stay with me! They are very rare, and I've been seeking a friend for Florrie ever since I found her. I want to let them go so they can have lots of Chameleon-mammal babies.'

'But Daddy!' Sir Peter whined.

'Either you leave them with me,' said Lord Florian, 'or you take nothing at all.'

Sir Peter pulled a face. '*Humph* ... alright then. But only if you keep the horrible cat. If he comes back with us, he'll jump up and down on the collection and ruin the whole thing.'

'Hang on a minute!' cried Captain Crank. 'That's my ship's cat!'

'If the cat comes with us,' said Sir
Peter, 'I'll moan all the way home.'

'That settles it,' Captain Crank
sighed. 'Lord Florian, the cat is yours.'

Toopo snuffled in his cage.

'I'll fetch Florrie,' said Lord
Florian, 'and introduce her to
everyone.'

'What shall I say?' Toopo whispered
to Scratch. 'I'm so scared!'

'Maybe tell her she's very clever-
looking and has handsome claws?'
said Scratch.

Toopo needn't have been scared.
When Florrie scurried in and jumped
on the table, she and Toopo both
turned pink at the same time, then
red, and then pink again.

'Hello,' snuffled Toopo through the bars of his bamboo cage. 'I've been looking for you all my life.'

'I've been looking for *you* all *my* life,' sniffled Florrie.

Toopo snuffled as Lord Florian opened his cage. Florrie sniffled as they both changed colour again. This time they turned pink with red spots.

Scratch just purred.

How It All Ended

Scratch sat on the bow of the *Petunia May* and watched the *South Seas Explorer* sail away. Captain Crank waved his handkerchief from the stern. He was happy to be going home so he could publish his maps of the Great South Land. Wal and Dave and Mick and Eric and Joe were happy too, because they hadn't seen

monsters or fallen off the edge of the
world. They were already preparing
the stories they would tell about the
ghost ship.

Sir Peter was nowhere to be seen. He was in his cabin, renaming all his father's specimens after himself.

Safe on the *Petunia May*, Toopo was happy because he would never have to sit inside a glass case. He and Florrie were allowed to run around on the ship, and when Lord Florian found an island with the right purple flowers, he was going to set them both free.

Scratch purred to himself. 'I'm still just a kitten, but I've done so many exciting things,' he thought. 'I've run away to sea. I've been a pirate cat. I've escaped from sharks and rocky reefs. I've saved a captain from the ice and I've hunted for treasure. And now I'm a ghost-ship's cat! I wonder what will happen next.'

He curled up in the sun and closed his eyes. 'There will be some new adventure over the horizon,' he purred. 'But right now, I'd rather have a snooze.'

And that's what he did.
Prrrr.

Words Sailors Use

cove	a small, sheltered bay
crow's nest	a small basket at the top of the mast, where a sailor could sit and look out for approaching land or danger
gangplank	a plank used for getting on or off a ship
hatch	an opening in the ship's deck, covered by a watertight lid
headland	a coastal cliff that sticks out into the sea
maroon	to leave someone behind on a deserted island as a punishment
mast	a stout pole rising straight up from the deck of a ship, which supports the yards and sails
porthole	a small round window on a ship
rigging	the ropes and chains used to move and support the sails on a ship
scupper	a drain hole on the deck
show your colours	fly a flag showing where your ship is from
starboard	sailor's word for 'right'
stern	the rear part of a ship
stow away	to sneak onto a sailing journey without the captain's permission
yardarm	either end of the pole at the top of a square sail